# BLIZZARD OF LOVE

## A MINNESOTA LAKES ROMANCE

### ROSE MARIE MEUWISSEN

BLIZZARD OF LOVE

BY

**Rose Marie Meuwissen**

Blizzard of Love

Digital/Print Edition
Copyright 2020 by Rose Marie Meuwissen
https://www.rosemariemeuwissen.com

ISBN: 978-1-954030-90-9
Published in the United States of America
Nordic Publishing
Edited by Mikayla Weeks
Cover Design by Rose Marie Meuwissen

nordic
PUBLISHING

❀ Created with Vellum

*To Cassie and a long ago ski trip when we had to drive through a blizzard to get there.*

A MINNESOTA LAKES ROMANCE

LAKE SUPERIOR

*Kari, a divorced mother of two teenage girls, was an independent woman determined to make it to Lutsen Ski Resort. Being a single mom hadn't been easy and left her little time to even think about meeting a man. This was a trip they'd all been looking forward to, they just hadn't planned on a snowstorm.*

*Being a dad full-time had only happened recently to Tyler, after his ex-wife decided to move out of state and dropped Matthew off on his doorstep, figuratively speaking. Owning his own construction company kept him too busy to even think about dating, but after running into Kari and her daughters, he was definitely rethinking that decision.*

*Stuck in a ditch with her two teenage daughters in the midst of a raging blizzard, forces Kari to realize her rescuer may be just the man to put her back on the road to love again.*

A MINNESOTA LAKES ROMANCE

MINNESOTA

**Land of 10,000 Lakes**

A MINNESOTA LAKES ROMANCE

*Blizzard Of Love*

by

*Rose Marie Meuwissen*

# CHAPTER 1

"*D*o we have everything?" Kari Sorenson asked her teenage daughters as she stared into the back of her black, mid-sized SUV. She wasn't even sure why she asked when she was pretty sure nothing else would fit.

"Yes, Mom!" Maddie and Tonia yelled in unison from the house.

Kari closed the rear door to the SUV and walked back into the garage to lock the door and set the alarm while the girls got into the back seats so they could watch a movie on the DVD player on the way. As she made her way back to the car, she glanced at the cloud filled sky. The weathermen were tracking a storm moving in from the West that was now in the Dakotas. Their predictions were the storm would swing low and probably only hit southern Minnesota. Of course, as far as she was concerned they never knew what they were talking about. In her opinion, based on the darkening sky and falling temperatures, they were in for a big snowstorm. But since she was heading up North, past Duluth, she felt sure they wouldn't get caught in it. After buckling her seatbelt, she backed out of the driveway and silently prayed they would make it to Lutsen.

It was over two hours to Duluth. The snow started falling about halfway there and kept on at a steady pace. The plows were out and the freeway was still clear when they reached Duluth, but unfortunately Lutsen Ski Resort was almost another two hours away.

"Maybe we should try to find a hotel and spend the night in Duluth," Kari suggested to her daughters.

"It looks bad out, Mom," Maddie said.

Kari pulled off the freeway and headed toward hotel row on the Duluth boardwalk. One after another, the hotel signs read, 'No Vacancy'. She noticed the worried looks on her daughter's faces, as she contemplated what to do. They couldn't spend the night in the SUV. It was too cold.

"We'll just have to keep on driving. Maybe once we get out of Duluth, we'll get lucky and find a motel with an available room. You girls keep your eyes open and watch for any vacancy signs."

"Okay," they answered.

Kari pulled back on the highway and headed north out of Duluth towards Lutsen. It was dark now and the giant snowflakes pelted her windshield so fast her wipers couldn't keep up. There were only a few cars still on the road, which could be either good or bad depending on how she looked at it. It lessened the chances of running into someone. Actually, sliding into someone was more like it. But then if she did end up in the ditch, there wouldn't be anyone to help her, either. She'd felt the tires start to slide more than once. The roads were slippery and the snow was getting deeper with each mile she drove. Thank heavens they were in a SUV with four-wheel drive.

"Mom, the signs all say, 'No Vacancy'," Maddie said.

Kari recognized the fear in Maddie's voice, revealing how

scared she was that they wouldn't make it. A full-blown blizzard raged around them as their SUV crept along the deserted highway. They were out in the middle of nowhere and couldn't turn back now even if she wanted to. She hadn't seen any cars on the road for a while. All she could do was try to drive down the middle of the road. Only problem was she could no longer tell where the middle of the road was, much less where the side of the road was, and where the road dropped off into the ditch. She was no longer sure they would make it either because they were currently in total whiteout conditions.

"Mom, I'm scared." Tonia's voice shook and Kari saw her tightly grip the armrest.

Every fiber of her being wanted to scream out, "Me, too." But she was the parent, the adult, and she would remain the strong one. It came down to sheer determination at this point, as she needed to make it to Lutsen Resort because she was deathly afraid of the alternative. She checked her phone to see if she had any bars, but there weren't any, which meant no cell service.

"Mom, look! I see lights behind us," Maddie shouted.

In the rearview mirror, Kari saw the faint light behind them, but wasn't sure it would be of any help to them. Although if it passed them, it would be easier to follow someone else's tail-lights.

# CHAPTER 2

*H*er eyes were glued straight ahead as she tried to determine where the sides of the road were. They only had thirty miles to go, but at this speed it would take at least an hour, and heaven help them if she stopped because she was pretty positive the car would never get going again. Then she felt it. The tug on the tire, dragging the car with it. They slid slowly and, knowing it was best not to fight it, she took her foot off the gas pedal. Off the road they went in only seconds, as she felt the car slide into the ditch. The girls screamed as the car came to a sudden halt with the passenger side now pushed up against a wall of snow. Thankfully, the airbags did not go off. Dazed, she heard her daughters crying. She could see them in the rearview mirror and could tell they weren't injured.

Was that knocking? She turned towards the driver's window and saw a man pounding on the glass. *He must be from the vehicle I saw behind us.*

"Are you okay?" he asked, his voice muffled through the glass.

She reached down to unlock the doors and pressed the

handle to open the driver's door. He opened the rear passenger door and leaned down to look into the backseat.

"Girls, are you hurt?" he asked.

"No," they answered.

"Good. Grab whatever you need and let's get you up to my truck."

Within minutes Kari and the girls were buckled into the strange man's pick-up along with his son.

"Were you headed to Lutsen Ski Resort?" he asked.

"Yes. And we almost made it," Kari stated.

"Yes, you did. Now let's see if we can all make it the rest of the way to some nice warm rooms at Lutsen instead of freezing to death out here."

He held his hand out to her. "Hi, I'm Tyler McClaren, and my son, Matthew," he stated, motioning towards the back seat.

She took his hand and said, "Kari Sorenson and my daughters, Maddie and Tonia. We are very grateful to you for rescuing us from the ditch. I don't know what we would have done if you hadn't been behind us." Her eyes glistened with moisture and she felt herself beginning to tear up.

Kari found herself staring into the dark brown eyes of an incredibly handsome man. He had high cheekbones and a sexy five o'clock shadow. He was damned good looking and still holding her hand. She hadn't held a man's hand for years. In fact, not since the divorce seven years ago. Actually, it had been quite a while even before then, since she'd really been with someone. Her ex-husband, Tom, hadn't been interested in spending time, much less being intimate, with her for over a year before she realized he was having an affair.

She released Tyler's hand when she heard someone clear their throat in the backseat.

Kari continued to study the man in the driver's seat. As he pulled his hat off, she noticed his coal black hair.

He turned towards her and smiled. "If anyone is into praying, now would be a good time. We're going to need all the help we can get." He stepped on the gas pedal and accelerated slowly. The wheels turned gradually, finally gripping the snow and moving them forward.

At this point, Kari was literally terrified. Hands clenched in her pockets, she stared out the window at the snow-covered road. There was still a good chance they wouldn't make it to the resort. If his truck ended up in the ditch, they would have no choice but to walk. At least they had warm jackets, ski pants and gloves. But still, it would be a long way to walk in this storm, even if it ended up only being a few miles. "Lord, please let us make it to the resort," she offered up in the form of a short prayer. *Oh and please let this guy be normal and not some crazy rapist or serial killer*, she added silently.

His son sat quietly in the back seat with Maddie and Tonia. The three teenagers didn't talk, just sat in dead silence. She thought she heard a stifled sob from her girls, and started to turn around to say everything would be okay, but thought better of it since she had absolutely no way of knowing if it would be okay or not. Instead, she glued her eyes to the road. If they were going to end up in the ditch again, she wanted to see it coming.

Finally, she saw the entrance sign for Lutsen. "Look! There's the sign. We're almost there!"

"We still have at least a mile to go," Tyler stated. "Their driveway is a long one. But it is a good sign."

Kari felt her tensed body relax. If anything happened now, they definitely would be able to walk.

Minutes later, they pulled up to the Lodge where check-in was located. When Tyler turned the engine off, loud sighs of relief could be heard from everyone in the truck.

"Let's get checked in so we can find out where our rooms are." Tyler got out and everyone else followed.

There was no one at the desk, so Kari rang the bell. A few minutes later, the clerk greeted them, checked them in, and handed them their room keys. Both of their rooms were in the last building on the road, closest to the ski hill.

They all piled back into the truck and proceeded down the entrance road to where it ended. Once everything was unloaded, everyone grabbed their bags and went inside. Their lodge numbers were on the sixth floor at the end of the hall. Kari and Tyler both stopped as they realized their rooms were across the hall from each other.

"I wonder if this is where our rooms were originally or if these were the only two they had left," Kari said. They each put the key into their lock and held the doors open as the kids walked inside.

"Mom, I didn't know you got us a fancy suite!" Maddie yelled back to Kari.

"I didn't." Kari released the door she was holding open and walked in to take a look. It definitely was a suite, with a separate bedroom, mini-kitchen, and pullout wall beds in the living room. Tonia had grabbed the door and was still holding it open as her head bobbed from one room to the other.

Kari walked back to the hallway and, after looking into Tyler's suite, realized the rooms were identical.

"Wow! I'm not complaining! This room is incredible and after what we both drove through to get here, we deserve this nice gesture. I don't have any issues with it."

Tyler stared into Kari's blue eyes. "I don't know about you, but I'm beat. Can't wait to get some sleep."

"Me, too. I'm absolutely exhausted." Kari turned to go,

and then abruptly pivoted back towards Tyler. "I just want to thank you for helping us. You very well may have saved our lives tonight. Who knows if anyone else would have come along or even noticed our car down in the ditch during this storm. We most likely wouldn't have made it to the resort by walking. Either way, trying to walk or staying in the car, we probably would have frozen to death. You are truly a hero in my eyes." Kari closed the short distance between them, wrapped her arms around his neck, and hugged him as tears rolled down her cheeks. Relief and joy intermingled in her body. A few seconds later, when she noticed that his arms had automatically embraced her in return, she realized she was hugging a strange man and hastily backed away from him. She looked into his eyes and saw that they were full of gentleness and compassion. "Thank you, again."

Tyler stood quietly staring at Kari. Finally, he said, "Not a problem. Anyone would've done it. Let's talk in the morning about getting your SUV out of the ditch."

Kari nodded and closed the door to her room.

# CHAPTER 3

*T*yler did the same. Being a single dad and running his own construction company took up all his time. Most of it, anyway. At least recently, he hadn't made any time for dating. In the early years after the divorce, he'd dated. But he'd been burned bad from his marriage and for a while hadn't been up to trying anything serious. Besides, he hadn't met anyone who interested him enough to even consider it. But Kari was a beautiful woman and only minutes ago was in his arms.

Then when Matthew hit his teen years, his ex-wife, Nadine, decided she wanted to move to a warmer state with her new husband. Feeling she'd put in enough years being a mother, she literally dropped Matt on his doorstep. She said it was his turn to be the parent. Not that he hadn't been there for his visitation times. He'd wanted to see Matthew more, but was limited to every other weekend due to his job. And that was what she wanted in the beginning after the divorce. He loved Matt and was glad to have him in his life full time, especially knowing he only had a few years left until Matt would graduate from high school and be off to college. That was why he and Matt were at Lutsen. It was the week after Christmas and Matt still had a week off before school started. Generally, this always was a slow week in the construction business, so here they were. Almost not making it to Lutsen in a blizzard.

With Kari . . . and her daughters.

He'd expected her thanks but hadn't anticipated finding her in his arms. She was a beautiful woman who was obviously fiercely independent, or she wouldn't have attempted the drive up to Lutsen in a snowstorm with her daughters. He hadn't expected the weather to get so bad since the weathermen predicted the winter storm wouldn't swing this far north. So she probably hadn't either.

He'd noticed her petite, trim body right away, and had always been a sucker for long, reddish blonde hair. And he wouldn't deny to anyone that it had felt good to have her body pressed up against his. The natural reaction to her body and the strong chemistry between them nearly compelled him to kiss her, and maybe he would've if there hadn't been three teenagers observing them. Yes, he was definitely interested in her, but hell he didn't even know for sure if she was single. All he had to say was, if she was married, the guy was an absolute idiot to let her drive to Lutsen today alone with his daughters.

Kari awoke to bright sunshine streaming through the slice of glass not covered by the closed curtain. The storm was over! She got up and walked to look out the window. There must have been at least a foot of snow on the ground. Everything was pristinely covered in white. In the bright sunlight, the snow glistened beautifully like sparkling diamonds. Why was it that after the storm, everything looked so beautiful, while during the storm, it was excruciating watching it fall so mercilessly to the ground?

An hour later, Kari, Maddie and Tonia made their way down to the restaurant in the lodge. Tyler and Matthew were already seated at a table and motioned for the trio to join them. The hostess directed Kari and her daughters to the table and added the additional place settings.

"Mom, look they have Swedish Pancakes," Maddie said pointing at the menu.

"Our grandma makes them for us whenever we stay at her house and I love them," Tonia added.

The waitress returned and took their order for three Swedish Pancake Combos.

The teenagers were all starving since they'd missed supper, and soon the table was filled with food. Tyler and Kari ate while observing their children conversing about the drive in the storm and the slopes they were anticipating skiing.

"I called AAA this morning about getting my SUV pulled out of the ditch, and they said they could probably have it towed to the resort by late this afternoon depending on how soon the roads were cleared," Kari said.

"Good. If they call you first and you'd like to be there when they pull it out, I can take you. Once they get it up to the road, you could drive it here. If it's drivable."

"That's a great idea. Are you sure you wouldn't mind?" she asked.

"Not a problem. The kids can go skiing while we meet the tow truck. I'm glad we moved the skis to my truck last night so the kids can hit the slopes in this fresh snow. The skiing will be exceptional," Tyler stated.

"Oh, I don't want to keep you from skiing today, too," she said.

"We have all week to ski. I'm happy to help a damsel in distress." Tyler smiled.

"Okay, I'll call them and ask them to give me a call when they're on their way to my SUV. Thanks again for helping me out."

"Mom, can we go to the room to change for skiing?" Maddie asked.

"Let me pay the check and we'll all go back," Kari said.

# CHAPTER 4

*A*n hour later they were at the ski lifts. Maddie, Tonia and Matthew headed up the hill on the lift while Kari and Tyler continued watching until they could no longer see them.

"Tyler!"

He heard his name and turned to see Dan, the father of Matthew's best friend, Jonathan. They were meeting up at Lutsen so the boys could spend the week together. He hadn't even thought to look for them since he hadn't heard anything from Dan. He assumed they'd decided to wait for the storm to pass and would come up today.

"Dan," Tyler said, walking over to him. "Did you just get here?"

"We were lucky and got a hotel room in Duluth last night, so we just arrived."

"Where are Emily and Jonathan?" Tyler asked.

"In the lodge getting us checked in," Dan said, pointing towards the building.

Then Dan looked over to Kari.

Tyler turned to make introductions. "This is Kari Sorenson. Her SUV slid in the ditch in front of me last night. Matt and I helped her and her daughters out of the vehicle and gave them a lift to Lutsen. We're just waiting for a call from the tow truck so we can meet them."

Dan walked over and extended his hand to her. "Nice to meet you."

Kari shook his hand. "Nice to meet you."

"Tyler, you and Matt still on for dinner tonight?" Dan asked.

"Definitely. We wouldn't miss it."

"We're meeting some other friends, too, and their teens for dinner about seven. If you don't have any plans, we'd love to have you and your daughters join us," Dan offered to Kari.

"I wouldn't want to intrude…" she hesitated.

"You wouldn't be intruding. Please join us. The Viking Room at seven."

"I'll think about it," Kari answered.

As Dan walked back to the lodge, her phone rang and she answered. After finishing the call, she said to Tyler, "The tow truck is about thirty minutes away from where my SUV went in the ditch."

"Okay, let's go meet it."

They walked over to Tyler's truck and got in. The roads had been plowed and salted, and looked good. There was still some snow packed onto the asphalt, but it was a hundred times better than the conditions the night before. There was an awkward silence, so Tyler turned on the radio.

"Why didn't your husband come up with you?" he asked, finally breaking the silence.

"We're divorced and he is always too busy with work to even take the girls on his weekends, so I just don't ask anymore."

"How long have you been divorced?"

"Seven years. The girls were quite young. Actually at a fun

age and he wouldn't even take them then. Now that they're teenagers, he doesn't want to deal with visitation at all because he doesn't really know them anymore. It's sad."

"Unfortunate for both him and your girls."

"How about your wife?" Kari asked.

"Divorced. Ten years. A few years ago she and her new husband moved to sunny Florida, and Matt wanted to finish high school here, so she dropped him off on my doorstep and left. Haven't seen her since."

"Must've been hard on him."

"He couldn't understand why she couldn't wait until he graduated. He's a junior at Chaska High School."

"My girls are at Lakeville South High School. Maddie is a junior and Tonia is a sophomore."

"Only a few years to go and we'll both be empty nesters, as they say."

"Yes. I try not to think about it," Kari said.

Just then, her SUV came into view, the front end sticking out of the snow up ahead. As they approached it, they saw a tow truck coming from the other direction and slowing down.

An hour later, her SUV was upright on the road. She thanked the tow truck driver, who already had all her info, as she opened the door to her SUV and got in. Thankfully, it started up right away. Tyler walked over to the driver's side and she pressed the button to lower the window.

"I'll follow you back to the resort. Just in case." He smiled as he walked back to his truck.

Tyler parked next to Kari when they arrived back at Lutsen. They got out of their vehicles and walked towards the lodge together. They'd told the kids to meet them back at the suites at four and it was almost three now. As they walked, Tyler watched the gentle sway of her hips in front of him. Once they reached the doors to their rooms, he asked, "You will be coming down to join us for dinner?"

"I really don't want to intrude on your friends. I already feel like I've taken up too much of your time."

"I didn't mind. I'd really like you to join us." He liked what he saw and wasn't about to take no for an answer. "Say yes."

"Okay. We'll meet you at the Viking Room at seven." She smiled and turned to go into her room.

# CHAPTER 5

*K*ari was attracted to Tyler, but it had been a long time. She had no idea how to flirt with someone or show she was interested in him. Her decision to not go had almost rolled off her tongue, but instead she'd agreed to go to dinner since his friend, Dan, had invited her.

When the girls returned from skiing, they talked nonstop about their day and how much fun it was. Especially to have a hot guy like Matthew with them. Oh and then, of course, all his friends were hot, too. So when Kari informed them they were all going to dinner together, they were ecstatic and went into a frenzy wondering what to wear.

Unfortunately, she hadn't really brought along anything to wear to have dinner with a man. And his friends. And a bunch of teenagers. She would have to see what she could put together that said "attractive divorced woman" versus "mom of teenage girls".

At six thirty, Maddie and Tonia announced they were finally ready, after changing clothes multiple times before finding something they deemed acceptable. Kari put on a pair of skinny jeans, a form-fitting, black sweater, a multi-colored, red scarf and her black boots.

They walked in and spotted Tyler at one of two tables set for ten. There were two other couples already seated with him. Matthew and a couple of other boys were seated at the other table. Tyler waved them over.

She hadn't realized the Viking Room was the high-priced dinner restaurant. It didn't really fit into her budget, but what price could she put on someone saving her and her daughters' lives? She could afford it for one night.

When they reached the table, Tyler got up and pulled out the chair next to him for Kari to sit down on and told the girls they could sit anywhere at the next table with Matt and his friends. Dan was seated across from Tyler next to a woman Kari assumed was his wife.

Tyler resumed his seat next to her. "Kari, you already met Dan, and this is his wife, Emily."

"Nice to meet you," Kari said.

"You are so lucky Tyler was behind you last night on the road. I don't even want to think about what might have happened," Emily stated.

"Me, either."

"This is Randy and Denise," Tyler continued with the introductions.

"Pleasure to meet you," Kari said.

The other two couples arrived a few moments later along with five more teenagers—three girls and two more boys. Tyler introduced the couples—Brad and Renee, Tom and Sadie.

The conversation at the adult table centered on the teenagers and what sports they were into, then moved to their plans for the week which consisted of skiing, snowboarding, snowmobiling, ice skating and snow tubing.

But as soon as the teenagers were done eating and had all

headed down to the rec room filled with video games, pool tables, ping pong tables, large screen TVs and old fashioned board games, bottles of wine appeared at the adult table and the conversation shifted to adult life, such as jobs, houses, and cars.

Emily asked, "What do you do, Kari?"

"I have a small business on the Internet. I take personal orders where I use themed t-shirts and picture scans to make custom keepsake quilts for special occasions like graduations, weddings and anniversaries. I get a lot of requests for sports team quilts, too," Kari answered.

"That sounds interesting! I may have to order one for my parent's anniversary. Do you have a business card with you?"

Kari reached into her purse, pulled out her cards, and handed them out, including one to Tyler. "If you go to my website, Nordic Quilt Designs, you can see the different designs we do."

Around eleven, the group decided it was time to go check on the teens and see if they could entice them to get some sleep tonight. Since the wine had kept coming, the dinner tabs had been left open. Kari watched the waiter drop off the checks and not give her one. She was about to say something when she realized hers was on Tyler's.

"I got it," he said and placed a credit card in the bill folder.

"You don't have to do that," Kari said, making eye contact with him.

"I know that. But I want to," Tyler stated and smiled at her.

At the rec room, they found the kids busy playing various games. Her girls were playing Twister with two of the boys. *Teens...*

"Maddie and Tonia, it's time to head back up to our room," Kari said.

"Please can we stay a little longer?" Maddie pleaded.

"Fine, but I want to see you at the room at eleven thirty sharp then," she said firmly.

"Okay," Maddie and Tonia answered together.

Kari walked back over to where Tyler stood watching.

"How about I walk you back?" he asked.

"Only seems appropriate since your room is across the hall," Kari laughed, and Tyler took her hand, leading her out of the rec room.

"I think we should take the long way back."

Kari followed him down the halls to a large area with a full-wall fireplace, where a robust fire roared. It was empty except for them. Tyler sat down on the couch in front of the fireplace, so she sat down beside him. It was too dang romantic. She was so attracted to him and it had been way too long since she'd been this close to a hot desirable man, which meant she could not be held responsible for her actions. Right? Focus, she needed to focus on what he was saying.

"I know you're divorced, but I have to ask, are you dating anyone?" Tyler asked.

They were facing each other and he was very close. His mouth was so near. She couldn't stop picturing him kissing her. What would it be like? She really wanted to find out.

"No," she finally managed to say.

That must've been the answer he was looking for, because he kissed her then. It had been way too long since she'd been kissed and Kari didn't want it to end. Her body's hormones were going crazy. She really needed to start dating again. What had she been thinking to not date? Waiting until the girls were off to college had seemed like a good idea. Yesterday, anyway. Tonight, it seemed absurd. She felt his lips move from hers. His hand reached up to her cheek.

"You're a beautiful woman, Kari." Tyler looked down at his watch. It read eleven–twenty-five. "We should probably get back to see if the kids listened to you." He stood and extended his hand to help her up.

"Yes," she managed to get out as they walked back to the rooms. When they got there, the girls and Matt stood chatting at the end of the hall.

Maddie looked at her phone and pointed at the time. "You're late, Mom."

"Very funny," Kari said as she unlocked the door.

Tyler unlocked his door, too.

"The lift at nine," Matt said as he walked into his room.

Tyler laughed. "I guess we're going skiing at nine. We'll see you then."

"Sounds good," Kari said and walked into her room, closing the door behind her.

# CHAPTER 6

*A*round ten the next morning, Kari found herself standing on top of Moose Mountain, the highest of the Lutsen Mountains, with Tyler. He was an excellent skier, while she was only at the intermediate level, so they chose the intermediate hills. The view of Lake Superior from the mountaintop was breathtakingly beautiful. The lake was a massive body of water and usually didn't freeze over. In fact, it had only frozen completely a couple of times through the years, she'd been told. Just a short distance from the frozen shoreline lay open water. A thick mist hung over the unfrozen sections of the lake.

"It's beautiful, isn't it?" Tyler asked, as if reading her thoughts.

"It's unbelievable. I've never been up here before." Even though she'd lived in Minnesota her whole life, she'd never managed to ski Lutsen before today. Kari was overwhelmingly happy to be there. For more reasons than one.

"Happy to know I'm your first," Tyler laughed.

The days flew by as the group of twenty took in all Lutsen had to offer. They skied every day amongst other things, and had dinner as a group each night. Kari got to know all the wives by the end of the week, and found she could easily become good friends with them. She intended to get together for lunch with the women when they got back to the Twin Cities.

After dinner on Saturday night, Tyler said he had a surprise for her. When they were done eating, he produced a women's snowmobile suit.

"And what's this for?" she asked.

"We're going to borrow Dan's snowmobile and I'm going to take you out for a ride. So put this on. Don't want you to get cold."

Maddie walked over. "Cool. A snowmobile ride." She looked at her mom, who seemed unsure from the look on her face. "Mom, you have to go. It'll be fun."

"Okay, but I don't want you girls to get into any trouble while I'm gone."

"Don't worry, Kari, we'll keep track of them. Go. Have fun." Emily gave Kari a reassuring look.

Thirty minutes later, they sat on the shore of Lake Superior, gazing at the frozen beauty of God's creation. A full moon shone brightly in the clear sky. Tyler left the snowmobile idling while they walked around. The temps had warmed up to the high twenties, so Kari wasn't cold in the snowmobile suit. She stood beside Tyler, gazing out over the frozen shore to the open water of Lake Superior in the moonlight. It was a moment to remember forever. Both stood in the eerie silence with only the gentle hum of the snowmobile behind them.

"It's so beautiful. Thank you for bringing me out here," Kari finally said.

"The night's perfect to see this and I wanted to share it with you." Tyler gazed into her eyes, then turned back to the snowmobile. He waved for her to get on behind him.

She got on and wrapped her arms around him as the snowmobile roared and skimmed across the snow back to Lutsen Lodge, where they removed their snowmobile suits and made their way inside.

Tyler took Kari's hand and pulled her through a door leading to a deck. He immediately took her in his arms and kissed her long and hard.

"I wanted to kiss you at the lake but we had too many damned clothes on." And then he kissed her again, like he would never let her go. Her body meshed against his. "I don't want this to end here. The thought of never seeing you again is driving me crazy. I'd like to keep seeing you when we get back home to the Twin Cities."

"I'd really like that," Kari said. "But it's really cold out here. Can we continue this conversation inside?"

Tyler kissed her again and they walked inside hand in hand. Once in the warmth of the lodge, he pulled Kari into his arms. "Now, would you like to continue the conversation or the kissing?" he asked softly into her ear.

Kari answered by stretching to press her lips against his and kiss him.

She'd set out last Saturday to spend the week skiing with her daughters. Along the way, they'd faced the possibility of freezing to death after their SUV ended up in a ditch during a blizzard. But luckily for them, a hero by the name of Tyler stopped to rescue them, and with his kiss gave her the hope of finding love once again.

To Kari, this weekend would always be remembered as "The Blizzard of Love".

*NOT THE END, BUT THE BEGINNING...*

# RECIPE

## NORWEGIAN / SWEDISH PANCAKES

*Fure Family Recipe*
Makes 20-25 pancakes

### Ingredients

- *1 ½ cups flour*
- *½ cup sugar*
- *6 eggs beaten*
- *2 cups milk*
- *4 Tbsp melted butter*

### Directions

- Beat eggs in large bowl until thick and light. Stir in milk. Add sugar and flour. Pour in butter.
- Heat large non-stick skillet pan until drops of water sizzle.
- For each pancake, pour 1/3 cup batter into pan, tilt pan so batter covers bottom.
- Cook 1-2 minutes or until bottom is lightly

browned, then turn. Continue cooking until
second side is lightly browned.
- Serve folded or rolled up with butter and berries.
Lingonberries are the preference for
Scandinavians.

# RECIPE PICTURE

*Norwegian / Swedish Pancakes*

# ABOUT THE AUTHOR

Rose Marie Meuwissen, a first-generation Norwegian American born and raised in Minnesota, always tries to incorporate her Norwegian heritage into her writing. After receiving a BA in Marketing from Concordia University, a Masters in Creative Writing from Hamline University soon followed. Minnesota is still where she calls home.

She has traveled around the world, including Scandinavia, but still has many places to see, enjoys attending Scandinavian events, writing conferences and is usually busy writing Minnesota Lakes Contemporary Romances, Viking Time Travel Romances or Norwegian Traditions Children's Books.

Visit her at www.rosemariemeuwissen.com or www.realnorwegianseatlutefisk.com.

NOVELS:

- *Taking Chances*—a contemporary romance novel set in Minnesota and Arizona.
- *Married by Saturday*—a contemporary romance novel set in Minnesota and Montana.
- *Looking for Mr. Right*—a contemporary internet dating romance novel set on Prior Lake in Minnesota—*Coming soon!*

NOVELLAS:

- *Annika—A Christmas Romance*—a contemporary romance set in Minnesota with a Nordic theme during the Christmas Holidays.
- *Skol! Viking Blonde Ale*—a contemporary romance set in Minnesota at an Autumn festival complete with a fortune teller, ale and Vikings!
- *Choosing to Live*—a Norwegian woman's journey during WWII to survive the Nazi Occupation of Norway—*Coming soon!*

# MINNESOTA LAKES ROMANCE NOVELETTES:

- *A Kiss Under the Northern Lights*—a Summer romance set in Ely, Minnesota on Big Lake.
- *Dancing in the Moonlight*—a Summer romance set in Malmo, Minnesota on Mille Lacs Lake.
- *Hot Summer Nights*—a Summer romance set in Prior Lake, Minnesota on Prior Lake.
- *Railroad Ties*—an Autumn romance set in Two Harbors, Minnesota on Lake Superior.
- *Blizzard of Love*—a Winter romance set in Lutsen, Minnesota on Lake Superior.
- *Nor-Way to Love*—a Spring romance set in Minneapolis, Minnesota on Lake Harriet.
- *Old Yule Log Fires*—a Christmas romance set in Excelsior, Minnesota on Lake Minnetonka.
- *A Date for Valentine's Day*—a Valentine romance set in Minnetonka Beach, Minnesota at the Lafayette Country Club on Lake Minnetonka.
- *Dance of Love*—a Fall Festival romance set at the Renaissance Fair in Shakopee, Minnesota.

CHILDREN'S BOOKS—

REAL NORWEGIAN'S SERIES:

- *Real Norwegians Eat Lutefisk*—a Children's book about the tradition of Lutefisk presented in both English and Norwegian.
- *Real Norwegians Eat Rømmegrøt*—the second Children's book in the series about the tradition of Rømmegrøt presented in both English and Norwegian.
- *Real Norwegians Eat Lefse*—the third Children's book in the series about the tradition of Lefse presented in both English and Norwegian.
- *Real Norwegians Eat Krumkake*—the fourth Children's book in the series about the tradition of Krumkake presented in both English and Norwegian—*Coming next!*

# MICRO-MINI NOVELETTE—COMING SOON!

- *Christmas Notes*—a collection of Christmas prose poems to warm the heart during the Christmas season.

CONTINUE READING FOR A
PREVIEW OF:

**ANNIKA—A CHRISTMAS ROMANCE**

*Betting on Paris Series*

*by*

**Rose Marie Meuwissen**

# ANNIKA—A CHRISTMAS ROMANCE

## COVER

ANNIKA—A CHRISTMAS ROMANCE

BETTING ON PARIS SERIES

ISBN 978-0-9903788-4-6
Published in the United States of America
Nordic Publishing LLC
Cover Design by Angie Speed

# INTRODUCTION

Spend the holidays with Josie, Ryley, Emma, Alana, and Annika. Get ready for five weeks of romance with a new Christmas series brought to you by five exciting contemporary authors...

BETTING ON PARIS SERIES

*Sometimes the best bet is the one you lose...*

Five best friends. Five promises.

Each year in mid-August, the former college roommates meet up on a girls-only trip somewhere in the world. This year, it's Paris, the city of museums, art and romance. On the last night of their vacation, the girls engage in a serious talk about the sorry state of their love lives and collectively decide they are swearing off men. Instead, each woman is intent on pursuing her life's goal. Falling in love is the *last* thing on her mind.

This is *Annika's* story...

Owning Nordic Travel and Tours was a dream come true and Annika certainly didn't have time for romance. So why had she met the man of her dreams, now?

Tristan's Minnesota Events and Adventures Company for singles allowed him the ability to meet available women on a regular basis, so why would he be interested in her?

Annika had never mixed business with pleasure before and since Tristan would be booking tours through her company, there would be no romance. Now, she only had to convince her heart.

*Find all the Betting on Paris novellas at Amazon!*

*Josie by Beth Gildersleeve*
   *Ryley by Donna Lovitz*
   *Emma by Angie Wilder*
   *Alana by Denise Devine*
   *Annika by Rose Marie Meuwissen*

After driving around the parking ramp for what seemed like an eternity, Annika pulled her SUV into an empty spot and quickly unloaded two medium-sized plastic tubs onto her wheeled cart, then hurried toward the glassed-in elevator. Plopping her purse down on top of the tubs, she pressed the button for the main level while her eyes focused on her phone to check the time. *Only thirty minutes until the doors open for the Minneapolis Travel Expo at the convention center.*

She took a couple of calming breaths, trying to erase visions of the backed up freeway she'd just spent way too much time on during the morning rush hour traffic. Thank God, she lived and worked in the suburbs! Absolutely no way, would she put herself through that rat race every day to get to work. The door opened and she backed out of the elevator pulling the cart with her, but stopped abruptly when she felt a firm pressure on her back. The top bin went crashing to the floor sending her travel brochures into a very messy pile beside her cart. She turned around quickly to see what had stopped her dead in her tracks.

Piercing blue eyes and sandy blond hair focused on her.

Her face flushed in embarrassment. "I'm so sorry. I'm in a hurry and wasn't watching what or who was behind me as I backed out of the elevator."

He grinned at her, sliding his phone into his pocket and bent down to retrieve a handful of brochures. "I can't let you take all the blame. I was on my phone and not paying attention to my surroundings, either. Let me help you." He picked up more of the fallen brochures and placed them into the plastic container.

Annika picked up the remaining brochures setting them in the bin, carefully placing the cover over the top, pressing down until she heard the click signifying it was on tightly. "Thank you. I do have to run though." She turned and quickly walked into the main ballroom with her cart in tow after flashing the security guard her exhibitor name-tag.

Thankfully, the booth had already been set up last night by her assistant, Holly, who would be arriving around noon after her prenatal doctor's appointment. Annika hadn't a clue what she would do without Holly for three months, maybe more, while she was out on maternity leave. The baby was due in October which was coming up way too soon.

They'd been late getting the newly designed brochures to the printer, only being able to pick them up yesterday afternoon which was why she'd been hauling them into the Expo this morning. She neatly arranged them on the table, and then sat down on the comfortably padded chair to reign in her emotions after her collision in the hallway. Typically, she didn't do things like that, but today she was off her normal routine after dealing with the traffic and rushing to get into the Expo before the event started and the doors opened. Well, she'd made it with a few minutes to spare. She picked up a bottle of water, left at the table for them by the Expo, and downed almost half of it, wanting to stay hydrated since she was about to do a lot of talking to potential customers and clients.

The guy she'd bumped into was definitely good looking, but she'd sworn off men for a year to concentrate on her business. Recently, on a trip to Paris with her best friends, Alana, Josie, Ryley and Emma, they'd all made a pact to focus on their jobs and to not let *any* men interfere with their career plans for a year. *Betting on Paris—No Men for a Year* was their pact slogan. Besides, her dream of owning her own travel tour company, Nordic Travel and Tours, had come true after the first of the year, when her boss, Dan Nystad, retired and sold it to her. Dan felt she was the best person to run the company and take it to the next step into the tech future of the twenty first century. He'd been a friend and mentor, teaching her everything about travel and tours for the past ten years of her career. She needed no distractions this year, especially, to make all the transitions needed to take her company into the new tech age, for which, it was sorely lacking.

At nine o'clock on the dot, the Expo's doors opened and people rushed in, eager to find all the freebies like pens, hats and bags, but hopefully there would be many who wanted to book tours and were serious about traveling in Minnesota and other places in the world, like Scandinavia, which was her specialty. Her booth would be giving away pens and brochures imprinted with photos of exciting cities and places to visit.

Soon, the aisles were full of people and many stopped at her booth to gaze at the breathtaking photos of the fjords of Norway on the promotional banners. Nothing could match their beauty. She handed out brochures and answered questions, trying to remember to take sips of water in between potential clients.

Holly arrived at noon carrying what appeared to be her lunch along with a large purse filled with necessities for the long day. "I made it." Holly sat down on the chair.

"I hope you didn't have to walk very far."

"No, I got a spot in the parking ramp, but at seven months pregnant any walking takes extra effort."

"Go ahead and eat your lunch and when you're done, I'll go get something from the food vendors."

Annika continued talking with the people walking through the Expo until Holly finished eating.

Holly stood up and walked to the counter. "I'm done so go ahead and get some lunch. Bet you didn't have any break-fast and are starving." She shooed Annika out of the booth.

Tristan watched the woman walk away. She definitely had poise and class, and appeared to be very professional. *Extremely attractive, too.* He was intrigued, but this was a work day and he was on a mission today. His Minnesota Events and Adventures Company, for singles seeking new friends and adventure in the Midwest and abroad, needed a tour company. Leisurely, he made his way toward the coffee kiosk, since the doors wouldn't open for another twenty minutes. He felt confident in finding the perfect tour company for his company's travel needs today, if his gut feeling was accurate and it usually was.

Finally, when the doors opened for the Expo, Tristan walked up to the counter and greeted Holly. "Hi, I think this might be exactly what I'm looking for." He picked up a brochure which oddly looked familiar.

"Well, that would make my job easier." Holly laughed.

"What can Nordic Travel and Tours do for you and your company?"

"My company is Minnesota Events and Adventures for singles. We set up events and travel destinations for our members. I'm looking for a company that can set up the tours and travel parts for us to sell as a group package to our clients. Basically, my company gets the people and your company would set everything up."

"This could be a perfect match because what we do is all the planning for trips such as the air, hotels, transportation and tours."

Tristan picked up a business card from the counter. "Are you Annika?"

"No, I'm Holly. Annika Karlstad is the owner and manager of the company and I'm her assistant." She pulled out her IPad with Annika's calendar. "I think you'd probably like to talk to her in person, so she can go over everything in detail. I have her calendar up on my IPad, so I'd be happy to set up an appointment next week for you."

Tristan pulled out his phone from his pocket and brought up his calendar. "Would Tuesday work?"

"She has a ten o'clock slot open."

"That should work." He pulled out his business card and handed it to Holly. "My name is Tristan Torgersen and I look forward to meeting Ms. Karlstad."

Holly smiled as she watched Tristan move on down the aisle past the rows of vendors.

Annika regretted not bringing a lunch when she saw the prices and the menu. Not that she had much choice at this point, so she ordered a salad and ice tea. While she waited for her food she checked her phone for any messages.

"So we meet again."

She turned to see who spoke. It was the man she'd literally run into earlier. "Hello. Again."

"How is the rest of your day going?"

"Much better. How about you?" Annika asked.

"Already made it half way through the auditorium. I think I've already found what I was looking for though."

"Oh, so will you still walk through the other half?"

"I'm here, so might as well take a look in case some other company strikes my fancy." Tristan chuckled.

"Well, best of luck…I guess I never got your name."

"Tristan."

"Well then Tristan, I'm Annika. Hope you find what you're looking for at the Travel Expo."

"I think I already may have found exactly what I'm looking for, Annika." Tristan smiled.

Annika heard her number called. "That's me. It's been nice running into you again." She gave him her best smile, then walked up to the counter to pick up her food. Discreetly, she positioned herself, so she could see if he'd left.

Tristan caught her eyes drifting his direction and tipped his head slightly in a nod, turned and walked back into the auditorium.

Why she felt so flustered around this guy, she had no idea. Her heart was racing and she knew she wanted to see him again. She knew nothing about him, so it was utterly ridiculous to be feeling this way. Besides, she wasn't looking for someone to date. At least not this year anyway, because she needed to stay focused on her company. She was personally responsible for making it a success. She didn't need any distractions.

After she'd finished eating her lunch, she made her way down a couple of aisles to check out the competition before going back to her booth. She felt confident about her company and what they had to offer clients. They offered bus tours to events and destinations in Minnesota and even some to the neighboring states of Wisconsin, Iowa, South Dakota and North Dakota. The tours to Scandinavia had always been top rated by their customers because they were unique in offering many off the beaten path options which were sought after by those with Scandinavian ancestry.

"Did I miss anything?" Annika asked taking a seat next to Holly.

"I put a couple of appointments on your calendar for next week that I think might be great new clients and handed out quite a few of the brochures."

"Tell me about the appointments."

"One is for a company looking to book some flight packages for their sales people who made their goals. And one is for the local company, Minnesota Events and Adventures. The company is for singles and they book group travel in and out of Minnesota for their events."

"Good job, Holly. Those sound like they have great potential for us."

A group of young people walked up to the table to ask about the trips to Iceland. Annika eagerly became engaged in conversation revolving around her passion for travel to the Scandinavian countries.